W9-BCQ-633

The Berenstain Bears GET THE DON'T HAFTAS

Stan & Jan Berenstain

Random House 🏠 New York

Copyright © 1998 by Berenstain Enterprises, Inc. All rights reserved under International and Pan-American Copyright Conventions. Published in the United States by Random House, Inc., New York, and simultaneously in Canada by Random House of Canada Limited, Toronto. ISBN: 0-679-89236-2 (trade) ; 0-679-99236-7 (lib.bdg.) Library of Congress Catalog Card Number: 98-65546 www.randomhouse.com/kids/   www.berenstainbears.com Printed in the United States of America   10 9 8 7 6 5 4 3 2 1 JELLYBEAN BOOKS is a trademark of Random House, Inc.

"It's quite a long trip to Aunt Dorothy's. I think it might be a good idea for you to go to the bathroom."

"I don't hafta."

"Now, we'll be leaving pretty soon.
And since we're already in the bathroom,
I think you ought to at least try."

"Papa and Brother are almost ready to leave, so this might be a really good time to go to the bathroom."

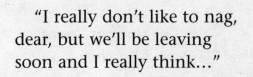

"I really don't like to nag, dear, but we'll be leaving soon and I really think…"

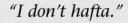

"I don't hafta."

"Hey, everybody!
Are we going to visit
Aunt Dorothy or not?"